Can you keep a secret?

Flower Wings are fairies with powers from flowers!

Flower Wings

Marigold Fairy Makes a Friend

By Elizabeth Dennis

Illustrated by Natalie Smillie

Ready-to-Read

SIMON SPOTLIGHT

An imprint of Simon & Schuster Children's Publishing Division • 1230 Avenue of the Americas, New York, New York 10020
New York London Toronto Sydney New Delhi
This Simon Spotlight edition February 2018 • Copyright © 2018 by Simon & Schuster, Inc.
All rights reserved, including the right of reproduction in whole or in part in any form.
SIMON SPOTLIGHT, READY-TO-READ, and colophon are registered trademarks of Simon & Schuster, Inc.
For information about special discounts for bulk purchases, please contact Simon & Schuster Special Sales
at 1-866-506-1949 or business@simonandschuster.com. • Manufactured in the United States of America 0518 LAK
2 4 6 8 10 9 7 5 3
Library of Congress Catalog Card Number 2017958411
ISBN 978-1-5344-1174-6 (hc)
ISBN 978-1-5344-1173-9 (pbk)
ISBN 978-1-5344-1175-3 (eBook)

Welcome to the land of the Flower Wings!

To most people, they just look like regular flowers. If you can see their wings, you are very special.

Meet Marigold Fairy!

She helps keep pests away

from the vegetable garden.

She also grows

big, tasty vegetables!

Marigold and Butterfly
are friends.

They do everything
together.

They cook together.

They eat together.

They even have the same favorite color.

They work together too.
When they see a pest
eating the vegetables,
they kindly ask it to leave.

"Shoo, please,"

Marigold says.

"Yes, shoo," Butterfly says.

Usually, that is all it takes

to make a pest go away.

Today they are going

to pick carrots.

There are orange carrots,

yellow carrots,

and even purple carrots.

"Oh no!"

says Marigold.

Then Butterfly says,

"Someone is eating

the carrots!"

"Is it a pest?"

Butterfly asks.

"It is a baby bunny!"

says Marigold.

"It eats a lot for a baby,"

says Butterfly.

"I am hungry,"

the bunny says.

"Pests ate our lettuce!"

Marigold feels her wings droop with sadness. She did not know that pests could have pests too.

"Can a pest be a friend?"

Butterfly whispers.

"Anyone can be a friend!"

Marigold decides.

Marigold uses her power to keep pests out of the bunny family garden.

"Now what will we eat?"

a snail asks.

Marigold does not want

anyone to be hungry,

not even pests.

"If you all agree to stop being pests," Marigold says, "we can teach you to grow lots of food!"

Now everyone grows

enough food to share,

and the pests are friends!

A double rainbow appears!

Thank you, Marigold Fairy!

Thank you, too, Butterfly!

The Science behind the Story

Did you know:
Farmers sometimes use marigolds in their fields, planting them in between rows of crops to keep pests away, just like Marigold Fairy does!

How it works:
The leaves of marigold plants have a strong scent that some say is unappealing to insects.

Butterflies and marigolds, best friends:
Butterfly and Marigold Fairy are friends in the story, but did you know that you can often find butterflies and marigolds together in nature, too? Butterflies are attracted to the bright colors of flower petals and need nectar for food. Marigolds are bright orange and yellow, and they are a good source of nectar throughout the year.

More about marigolds:
For centuries, different kinds of marigolds have been used to make dye for yarn and fabric!